For Fiona, story-spinner extraordinaire
M. M.

For Papa Rudge and Mama Lou
L. R.

Text copyright © 2011 by Meg McKinlay
Illustrations copyright © 2011 by Leila Rudge

First U.S. edition 2012

Library of Congress Cataloging-in-Publication Data is available.

Library of Congress Catalog Card Number pending

ISBN 978-0-7636-5890-8

16 15 14 13 12
SCP 10 9 8 7 6 5 4 3 2

Printed in Humen, Dongguan, China

This book was typeset in Kosmik and Mrs Eaves.
The illustrations were created digitally.

Candlewick Press
99 Dover Street
Somerville, Massachusetts 02144

visit us at www.candlewick.com

NO BEARS

MEG McKINLAY

illustrated by

LEILA RUDGE

CANDLEWICK PRESS

Hi! I'm Ella, and this is my book.

You can tell it's a book because there are words everywhere.

Words like

and *Happily ever after*

and **The END.**

I'm in charge of this book, so I know everything about it — including the most important thing, which is that there are **NO BEARS** in it.

I'm tired of bears. Every time you read a book, it's just **BEARS BEARS BEARS** — horrible furry bears slurping honey in awful little caves.

You don't need **BEARS** for a book.

You need **pretty** things.

You need **fairies** and **princesses**

and **castles**.

You need **funny** things,

exciting things,

and **scary** things—

maybe a **monster**

or a **giant** or something.

Hmm, yes. I like the sound of that.

So, how about this?

Once upon a time

there was a beautiful princess.

The princess lived in a faraway castle with her father, the king, and her mother, the queen, and her fairy godmother, the fairy godmother.

But **NO BEARS**.

NOT

EVEN

ONE.

Yes, perfect! This is my kind of story. So...

There were **NO BEARS** in the castle, and there were **NO BEARS** in the village. There were **NO BEARS** in the whole entire kingdom or the next one or the next one.

There were **NO BEARS** in the deep, dark forest in the faraway lands.

But what there **WAS** in the deep, dark forest in the faraway lands was . . .

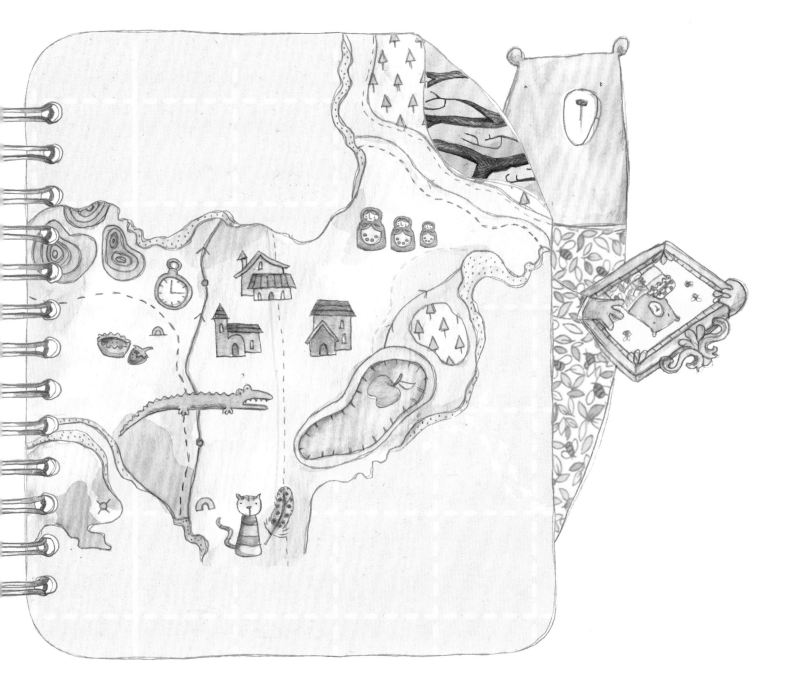

A MONSTER!

An evil, terrible monster who wanted to steal the princess away so she could read him bedtime stories every night.

Ooh. This is getting scary.

One day, the monster set out from the faraway lands.

He climbed a mountain.

He crossed a river.

He stomped through one kingdom

and the next one

and the next one.

He crept through the village and up the stairs and into the castle . . .

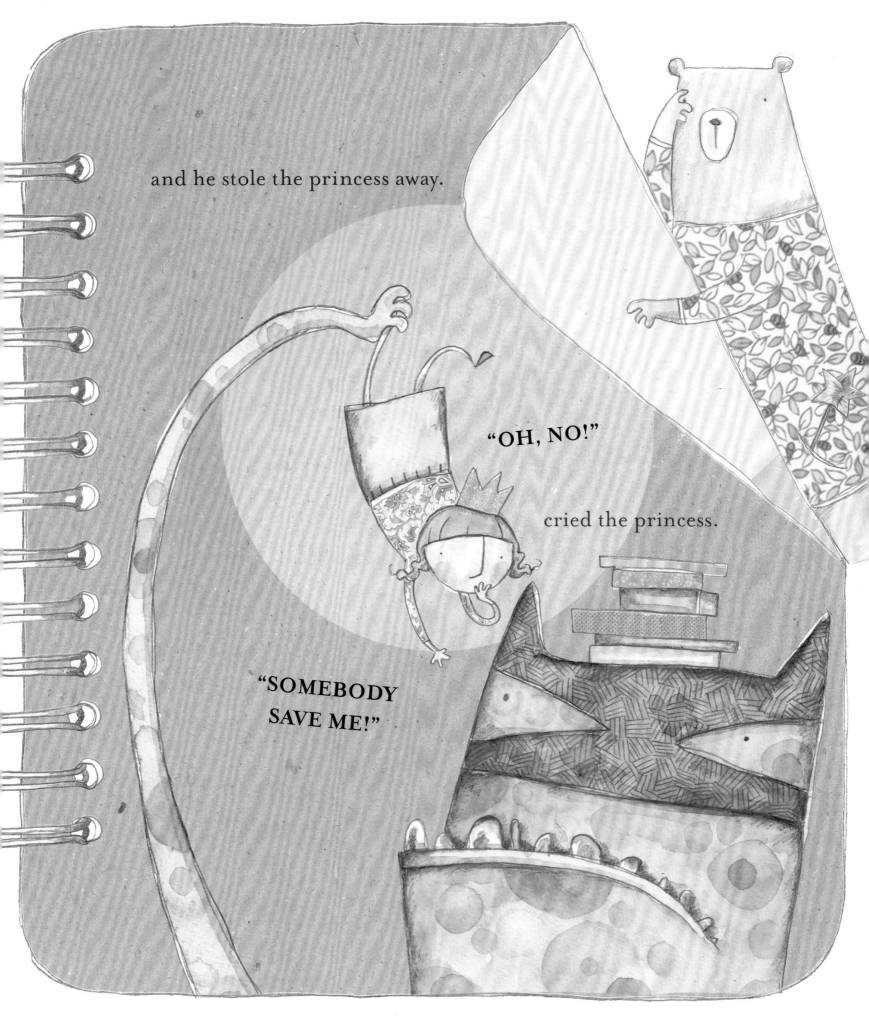

and he stole the princess away.

"OH, NO!"

cried the princess.

"SOMEBODY
SAVE ME!"

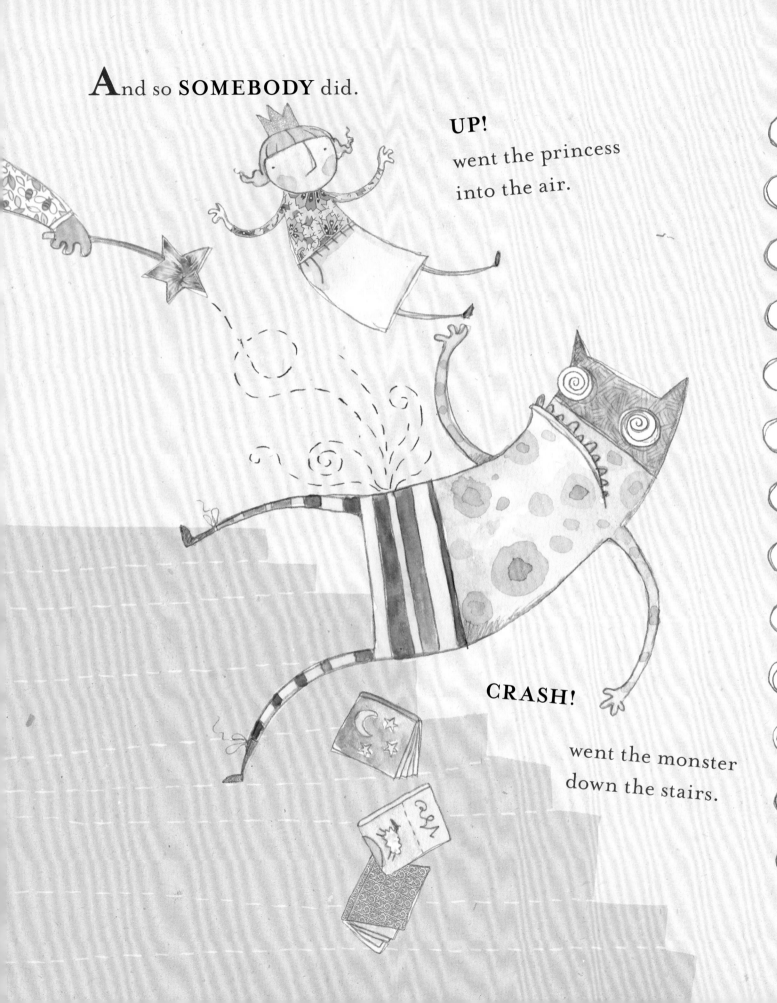

And so **SOMEBODY** did.

UP!
went the princess
into the air.

CRASH!
went the monster
down the stairs.

DOWN!

came the princess,
safe in the tree.

SPLASH!

went the monster
into the sea.

Phew! That was close.

"Hooray!" cried the princess. "I'm saved."
Then her father, the king, and her mother,
the queen, threw a party for the fairy godmother.

Because everyone knew she was the one who had saved the princess with her fantastical magic powers.

Wow! This turned out to be a pretty good book, don't you think?

In fact, I think this has been the prettiest, most exciting, scariest, and funniest book ever.

And I know why!

Because there were **NO BEARS** in it.

NOT ONE!

So now there's only one thing left to do.

And I think you know what that is.

It's to say that everyone lived

happily ever after.

The
END